ALL I CAN SEE

JOYCE BLOOM

Remez Press

New York, New York
www.remezpress.com

ALL I CAN SEE Copyright © 2006 by Joyce Bloom.
All rights reserved. No part of this book may be used or reproduced in any manner whatsoever, without written permission from the author or publisher except for the inclusion of brief quotations in critical articles or reviews.

Library of Congress Control Number: 2006921083
Bloom, Joyce.
　All I Can See:

ISBN 0-9-777784-0-1

Remez Press
P. O. Box 20053
New York, New York 10021-0060
www.remezpress.com

Cover art by Michael Esguerra, M. E. Graphic Design
Printed in the U.S.A.

*For my grandparents,
Isaac and Pauline Hellreich;
their sight was straight and clear.*

Acknowledgements

My deepest appreciation goes first to my mother Rita Hellreich Bloom and my father Harold Bloom, obm, for providing me with the courage to see and to write. My gratitude goes to my teacher and guide, Rabbi Shloma Majeski, who has helped me to learn the fundamentals of seeing further and deeper.

My special thanks to Mrs. Judith Bleich for her generous editing, friendship, support and time—which seems to stretch for her.

To Sondra Blum Suskind, wherever she is, I offer my true gratitude for her friendship and personal assistance, especially during the time that this story was unfolding within me.

And my sincere appreciation goes to all of the many other friends and relatives who have assisted me, without whose help this endeavor would not be what it is.

A Note to My Readers

This story is my story and your story.

It's a story that, like all fables, lends itself to illustration. Yet, I have not illustrated it or had it illustrated. Since this story is as much yours as mine, I felt that illustrating it would lock you into what I see and that's not good enough. This story should help you see what you can see. And so, the book has been printed with the left side pages purposely left blank. Those of you with an inclination to draw or doodle can use that space to actualize your perceptions or feelings as you go along on this journey. For those of you who don't draw, you'll have the space to conjure up your own mental images without someone else's interpretation.

If you wish, you can send your sketches, illustrations or doodles to: www.remezpress.com, where they will be viewed by me and may be posted to share with other readers. I will be interested to see your interpretations.

Wishing you a smooth passage.

There once was a beautiful fragile butterfly whose wings were bespeckled with all the colors in the rainbow. She was a long time sleeping in her cocoon when at last she emerged to live in a green land where all the flowers were red. As she came out of her cocoon, she smelled the air and stretched her beautiful bespeckled wings, feeling free at last.

She flew all over the green land stopping now and again to rest on a red flower. She looked at all the land and all that was upon it. She wanted very much to see all that she could see. And everywhere she looked she saw the land was green and all the flowers were red, and all the butterflies had bespeckled wings, but there was no other with all the colors of the rainbow, as she.

Each day she flew further and further from the place where she first left her cocoon because she wanted very much to see all that she could see.

One day she came upon a bee. "What thing are you, that flies but is not a butterfly? she asked. "I am a bee," he replied. And then he asked, "What are you doing here? You are a beautiful fragile butterfly. There are no butterflies here," he said. "I am flying around to see what I can see. So long was I in my cocoon and now I am free. Please, Mr. Bee, you seem wise and must have traveled far, will you tell me, what did you see?" And the bee replied with a sigh, "Yes, I have traveled long and far and wherever I have been and wherever I go, I see me."

Now the beautiful fragile butterfly thought this a very strange answer as it made no sense to her, at all. She thought perhaps the bee was making fun of her because he had traveled far and she didn't even know that he was a bee. But she thanked the bee anyway and set off again to see all that she could see.

Soon she forgot the bee and his strange words.

The scenery changed and the land was brown instead of green and the sky was dark and the beautiful fragile butterfly was cold and afraid.

But the beautiful fragile butterfly flew on ahead, further and further into the brown land, until she spied something that looked like a flower.

In fact, it was a flower, but the beautiful fragile butterfly wasn't sure because in her land all the flowers were red and this thing which seemed to be a flower, and which in fact was a flower, was blue.

And the beautiful fragile butterfly took a chance and rested all the night long on it.

In the morning she felt good, the sun was shining and there was another butterfly nearby on another blue flower.

Now, the other butterfly was as brown as the land. He stood poised on his hind legs on the nearby blue flower looking oddly at the beautiful fragile butterfly. The beautiful fragile butterfly, glad for the company, flew over to the brown butterfly, but just before she reached the blue flower that he was on, the brown butterfly flew off of it and alit on yet another blue flower only a breath away from where the beautiful fragile butterfly had now landed.

As the brown butterfly continued to stare questioningly at her, the beautiful fragile butterfly asked him, "Are you from this land? Have you traveled far? What did you see?" And the brown butterfly, taken completely aback by the direct questioning by the beautiful fragile butterfly whose brilliant speckles so bedazzled him, answered as though entranced, "Yes, I am from this land, but no, I have not traveled beyond my land, and here I see only me."

How strange, thought the beautiful fragile butterfly, this brown butterfly answers just like the bee, yet, he has been nowhere. "Shall I tell you about my land?" asked the beautiful fragile butterfly, wanting to be friendly. "Yes, please do," said the brown butterfly, from the brown land with the blue flowers, still somewhat bedazzled by the rainbow of speckles before him.

And the beautiful fragile butterfly began; "All the land is green and all the flowers are red, and ..." But, at this last, the brown butterfly opened his eyes wide and interrupted the beautiful fragile butterfly by saying, "Don't be silly, flowers can't be red, all the flowers are blue. I have seen some of my land is green too, but positively flowers can only be blue."

The beautiful fragile butterfly tried very hard to explain that the blue flowers of the brown land seemed to be the same as the red flowers of the green land but the brown butterfly only got angry and turned away from the beautiful fragile butterfly and finally, without even saying goodbye, flew away.

Now the beautiful fragile butterfly was completely confused by the behavior of the brown butterfly, and she just sat on the blue flower where the brown butterfly had originally been, shaking her head, until she realized that she was cold again. But this time it was still early morning and the sun was shining, so the beautiful fragile butterfly fluttered her bespeckled wings and flew on, ahead, across the brown land, to see all that she could see.

At last she arrived at the sea.

What is this? she thought; no land, no flowers, only rain, lots of rain lying on the ground. The rain went on and on and she couldn't see the other side.

Fluttering at the edge of the water, the beautiful fragile butterfly considered her position. The sun is still shining and I do want to see all that I can see, I will fly ahead, out over this rain that is lying on the ground to see what there is to see.

And the water stretched on and on.

Now after awhile the beautiful fragile butterfly became tired and hot. The sun was shining ever more brightly than it did in her land or in the cold brown place she had just come from where she met a brown butterfly and where she rested on blue flowers.

There were no flowers of any color on the rain beneath her. But the beautiful fragile butterfly was not afraid. She had seen rain on the ground before (although not so much in one place) and the beautiful fragile butterfly decided to stop on it for a moment to rest.

But as her delicate feet touched the water she became afraid. She could not stand. There appeared to be no ground under the rain and the water was moving very fast. The beautiful fragile butterfly was afraid she would be pulled under the flow. Quickly she flew up above the water and circled frantically, looking in all directions to see if she could find some safe place to rest.

As she looked around, a fish came to the surface.

Now the fish was half out of the water in the center of the circle in which the beautiful fragile butterfly was frantically flying, and all around him was a dark ring on the water. "Why are you making strong shadow over this area?" he chafed.

"What? Strong Shadow?" she stammered. And the beautiful fragile butterfly was so startled by the appearance of the fish below her that she breathlessly continued, "I am tired and I can't rest on this rain. There are no flowers here. I have flown without rest from the brown land with the blue flowers now behind me."

"Are you of the brown land then?" the fish interrupted, still indignant.

"Oh no, I'm from the green land where all the flowers are red. I am traveling around to see what I can see. So long was I in my cocoon and now I am free."

Now while the fish and the beautiful fragile butterfly were talking, the ring that was on the water and that encircled the fish began to fade.

And the fish smiled a big knowing smile at the beautiful fragile butterfly and said, "Come, young one, light on my head for a time. You can rest and I shall tell you of shadows and of this water that you mistake for rain."

And the beautiful fragile butterfly, hot and exhausted, flew back down toward the dangerous water. She stepped onto the fish just above his mouth and relaxed her weary bespeckled wings on his wrinkled face.

And the beautiful fragile butterfly and the fish looked into each other's eyes.

And in the eyes of the fish, the beautiful fragile butterfly saw the sky above and what she thought was a glint of the sun. The fish's eyes were large, each larger than the beautiful fragile butterfly when her bespeckled wings were at full span.

In a moment the fish began to speak. And the words floated up, from his mouth that was behind her, creating a cooling breeze.

"A shadow" the fish began, "is a tract of partial darkness produced by a body intercepting the direct rays of the sun. It obscures. Of course it can also screen, or protect. Ah, indeed a shadow can be a beautiful thing. But, you were making strong shadow," he admonished, "and that is not good at all. You circled round and round this spot breaking its contact with the sun, over and over, changing the flow. You must know, little one, it is not good to break the flow, and especially not by creating strong shadow."

And the beautiful fragile butterfly looked quizzically into the big fish eyes. "Your words are very strong for me," she said. "I just wanted to find a place to rest, and now I have found one on you."

"Will you tell me of the rain that is not rain?" she asked, changing the subject.

And the fish laughed from behind her at the obvious ploy, and complied.

"This is not just rain" said the fish, "this is the sea."

"The sea" instructed the fish, "is a huge body of water. The water is salty, not like rain at all. All around it is land that has risen from the land that is deep beneath the sea. There are many species of fish and flora and fungi and such in the sea."

"But why are there no flowers?" asked the beautiful fragile butterfly. "Ah, but there are flowers," the fish replied, "wonderful flowers, flowers of every color, on the land deep below the water. Would you like to come down to see them?"

And the beautiful fragile butterfly thought for a moment, then said, "No. Thank you. I must continue on my way across this rain that is not rain but a sea. Please tell me, have you been to the other side? What did you see?"

And the fish laughed again, this time coming a little further out of the water. And the beautiful fragile butterfly fluttered her wings, bespeckled with all the colors in the rainbow, to keep her balance on the fish.

And the fish replied as the sun played in his eyes, "I have been to all sides of the sea, and everywhere I see me."

This is just too strange thought the beautiful fragile butterfly. First the bee, then the brown butterfly from the brown land with the blue flowers, and now the fish from the rain that is not rain but a sea, all said, "I see me."

But the beautiful fragile butterfly decided not to question the fish anymore because the sun was going down and she didn't want to be on the water at night.

She thanked the fish for his kindness and, well rested, flew off, ahead toward the other side of the sea.

She sailed ahead across the rain that was not rain but a sea. And she looked at the water and saw all that was upon it. She saw the sky in the water and could chart her course and scout the way ahead as she peered at the topography beneath her. She saw the water in constantly moving peaks and valleys. The water rocked and rolled and splashed and splayed. There were areas where the water seemed to be still only to be hiding swirling, hypnotic eddies. She saw bubbles and foams. She saw clouds that took on strange shapes she had never seen and shapes of things she had seen before. She saw the sun.

The sun doesn't set, she realized suddenly. Something was wrong. The further she flew, the longer the day lasted. This is some trick she thought, and she raised her head to check the sky.

The sun was still high in the sky. She knew it was mid morning where she was but her body was acting as if it was late afternoon. Time has changed she thought and was immediately startled by the thought.

She shook her head. Nothing changed. Well, I am not really tired and that confusing fish is not here anyway, she thought obstinately. This is good for me, because I don't want to fly, in the dark, over this rain that is not rain but a sea.

And she flew ahead, across the sea, on and on and on, thinking nothing more about her recent exchange with the fish or the sun that didn't set, but now she watched both the sky and the water carrying with her head the completion of a wave to the sky then back to the water for a new wave to follow.

At last she reached the shore.

She flew over the last waves of the rain that was not rain but a sea, to where the water teased the land now reaching forward, now pulling back. And the beautiful fragile butterfly thought, I am going mad. The day is endless. The sun does not set. I see no flowers from the farthest reach of the water. The land is orange and black and it stretches like a roller coaster maze to the sky. Where am I?

But suddenly she realized that she was flying up and back over the same spot and making the strong shadow again that the fish had warned her against. So she drew in a deep breath and flew out, ahead, over the orange and black land beyond the tide.

She flew and flew and everywhere the land was orange and black, and the day did not end. She stopped to rest, hop-scotching from black peak to black peak to black peak, never staying on any one too long, afraid of the hideous noise they emitted. And the orange and black maze stretched before her as far as she could see.

And the beautiful fragile butterfly was lonely and confused and she started to cry as she flew down toward yet another black peak.

When, through her tears, the beautiful fragile butterfly spotted movement in the sky.

At last, a bird, she thought. She had seen birds flying in the green land with the red flowers. From the distance she could tell it was too big to be a bee or even another butterfly. It must be a bird. And the beautiful fragile butterfly forgot her tears and now flew smiling forward.

Now, the bird she saw was gray everywhere. His feathers were gray and fine as silk and formed a ridge around his head that formed the base of the pyramid which was his crown. His beak was gray and wide and stretched out to form a pyramid half the size of the crown. His body was gray and sleek and his legs were thick as a cat's with paws and six claws fitted for grip. His wings were gray down shaped like harps. His eyes were shaped like diamonds. His eyes were gray. The bird she saw was gray everywhere.

"Hello," said the beautiful fragile butterfly. "I am so glad to see you. I have traveled very far. I am tired. I want to rest but I can't find any flowers in this orange and black maze of a land and the black peaks make such a hideous noise. Can you tell me where are the flowers?"

And the bird chirped a hideous song, no two sounds alike, no melody, nothing like anything the beautiful fragile butterfly had ever heard a bird say before. It was frightening but somehow familiar.

As the beautiful fragile butterfly just fluttered in the air staring at the bird as long as he spoke, he realized that she did not understand him any more than he had understood her, so he motioned for her to follow him and started off toward yet another black peak.

Now the beautiful fragile butterfly did not want to go to another black peak, so she fluttered her bespeckled wings and flew away from the strange gray bird and the black peaks.

Of course, the gray bird did not understand her words, but he did understand that she didn't want to go to the black peak with him so he began to fly off in another direction again signaling the beautiful fragile butterfly to follow him.

And she did.

The beautiful fragile butterfly looked at the orange and black land all around her and at all that was upon it.

The strange gray bird led her in a more or less straight path, between black peaks where possible and through them where there were passages she had not noticed before.

They flew for only a short while, but they covered a great distance.

Now before them lay a patch of purple, covered with clumps of tiny white flowers. The beautiful fragile butterfly wasn't sure they were flowers because they were white, but she had seen blue flowers in the brown land and the fish had told her there were flowers of all the colors in the rainbow beneath the sea, and the flowers of her own green land were red and she was so very tired, that she took a chance and flew straight down to the purple patch and alit on a tiny white flower without even a glance at the hovering bird who had led her there.

And the beautiful fragile butterfly found the tiny white flowers very soft.

And the beautiful fragile butterfly looked at the strange gray bird now hovering close above her and smiled. And for a moment it seemed as though the speckles in her wings danced with the sun in the sky. And she said to the strange gray bird, "Thank you ever so much. I was so very tired." Then she remembered that the strange gray bird did not understand her language, and she paused. And the strange gray bird squawked his hideous noises at her and took off to fly around the patch.

Now the beautiful fragile butterfly, alone on the tiny white flower closed her eyes and fell almost immediately to sleep even though it was still light and she had never slept in the light before.

This time while she slept she dreamed and her dream had many colors, green and red and brown and blue and orange and black, and all the while she slept on the tiny white flower in the purple patch amidst the orange and black land. And all the while the strange gray bird hovered over her and flew around the patch and hovered over her and flew around the patch.

And when the beautiful fragile butterfly awoke, she found the strange gray bird hovering over her.

And the beautiful fragile butterfly felt warm in the light that had not waned, and safe with the strange gray bird even though he sounded so very harsh.

Some time while the beautiful fragile butterfly slept the strange gray bird had thought to bring some food for her. And soon after she opened her eyes, she looked up and found him directly above her. At once, the strange gray bird swooped down to the tiny white flower and offered her a worm.

Now the beautiful fragile butterfly did not eat worms but she also did not know if they were good or bad or what they were, because she had never seen any worms before. And the strange gray bird sensed that she did not know what the worm was for, so he ate half to show her that he intended to give her food, and how to eat it.

But the beautiful fragile butterfly's mouth was not made for eating worms and not knowing what else to do she just sat on the tiny white flower in the purple patch amidst the orange and black land and looked helplessly up at the bird. And the strange gray bird looked helplessly at the beautiful fragile butterfly and saw that she could not eat the worm. In his hideous sounding language he said, "Okay, I will bring you something else. What would you like? What do you eat? I don't know for I have never seen anything like you before. You are beautiful and fragile and I can see that you are tired and hungry. Let me help you. I will make you mine."

And even though the beautiful fragile butterfly did not understand one word of what the strange gray bird had said, she knew even through the hideous sound of his language that he meant to help her, and she noticed that he didn't sound quite as bad as before her rest.

And the beautiful fragile butterfly replied in her own language, the language of the green land with the red flowers, "I can nibble on the white flower and, if it is good, I will have plenty of food. I cannot eat the worm, for my mouth was not made for eating worms but thank you for bringing to me what you thought was good food."

And the beautiful fragile butterfly bent to nibble at the tiny white flower.

And it was good.

And the beautiful fragile butterfly rested on the tiny white flower which was her bed and her food, safe and content, beneath the shade of the wing of the strange gray bird.

Again the strange gray bird did not understand her words but he did understand her action and her smile of contentment and the strange gray bird was happy that she had food. He was happy to see the beautiful fragile butterfly and to be near her, and he put his wing over her to shade her from the light which never grew dim.

And the beautiful fragile butterfly was happy.

Now after some time, the beautiful fragile butterfly was completely rested and even a little restless because she wanted to see all that she could see.

So she fluttered her wings and the strange gray bird, alert to her movements, knew that she was finished resting and flew up ahead of her to make sure the way was safe. They flew together between and through the black peaks, and all the while, the strange gray bird was talking his hideous sounding language.

And the beautiful fragile butterfly began to understand.

And everywhere the land was orange and the peaks were black, and the strange gray bird always darted in more or less of a straight line.

HAQUI BERAQUICK!" screeched the strange gray bird as he saw the beautiful fragile butterfly heading into a collision with a black peak.

And the beautiful fragile butterfly was startled as out of a dream. She had been drifting.

She looked around her. She was in the orange and black land, orange and black everywhere. She flew more cautiously and watched the strange gray bird more closely and listened to his constant chatter.

Many times they flew together out over the orange and black land and each time they flew together back to the purple patch with the tiny white flowers.

And the sun did not set.

Now one day when the beautiful fragile butterfly awoke beneath the shade of the wing of the strange gray bird, she said to him in his hideous sounding language, "You are very kind, and gentle and good and I am very happy here with you. You have shown me the orange and black land but now I must return to the green land with the red flowers."

And the strange gray bird was very sad.

And the beautiful fragile butterfly was very sad.

"Why must you go? You are beautiful and fragile and I want to keep you with me," lamented the strange gray bird. And the beautiful fragile butterfly did not answer for a long time. "I will wait a little longer" she said at last, because she really did not know why she had to go.

And every day the strange gray bird showed the beautiful fragile butterfly the orange and black land and every night although there really was no night, for it never got dark, they returned to the purple patch with the white flowers, so the beautiful fragile butterfly could sleep on a white flower bed beneath the shade of his wing.

Now one day while the beautiful fragile butterfly was resting, the strange gray bird swooped down from his position above her for a chat.

He told her that he would like to take her into one of the black peaks where he would introduce her to some other gray birds who were his friends.

And the beautiful fragile butterfly thought to herself, other birds in the black peaks, of course. And she realized that the hideous hum of the black peaks that still frightened her was just the sound of other birds.

And she flashed another of her smiles which lit up the rainbow that was her wings, and said to the strange gray bird, "I would love to go."

The beautiful fragile butterfly wanted to see all that she could see.

And the strange gray bird stretched his wings and resumed his position above the beautiful fragile butterfly.

And the strange gray bird was happy.

And the beautiful fragile butterfly was happy.

And after some time the beautiful fragile butterfly and the strange gray bird flew off, making their way directly through the orange and black land until they came to an opening in one of the black peaks. Instead of flying through it, the strange gray bird turned upward and entered a brightly lit maze inside the black peak, open to the sky.

Now it took the beautiful fragile butterfly and the strange gray bird some time before they stopped because there were many wall-like partitions that they had to circle around. They moved left and right and forward and back to make their way inside the black peak. There were many gray birds everywhere they turned and all the birds they saw were squawking and screeching the hideous sounding language.

Finally, they stopped at a group of six gray birds.

Now the six birds who were the friends of the strange gray bird squawked and gestured too, and they flew up and down and all around the area in a frenzy of welcome. They made every effort to make the beautiful fragile butterfly comfortable, but there were no tiny white flowers upon which she could rest. And now the strange gray bird who was her friend squatted alongside her so she was unshielded from the light which streamed endlessly into the black peak.

All of the strange gray birds made such a fuss over her. They had never seen anything like her before. And they were all very friendly and polite to the strange gray bird who was her friend. So she found a shelf about eye level with the birds and perched precariously on it while they talked in the hideous sounding language she had begun to learn.

And the strange gray bird was happy.

And the beautiful fragile butterfly was happy.

Only the birds seemed to like to stay in the light all the time and here there were no white flowers, and the ground was a dusty gray ash that made the air thick, not at all like the ground in the purple patch which was so much like the green ground of her land, and all of the birds were squawking and squealing and screeching at once, so she could hardly understand what they were saying. But she could see that the strange gray bird who was her friend was happy.

Now the beautiful fragile butterfly eventually grew tired and hungry.

And the strange gray bird who was her friend saw that she was tired and hungry and got up to leave the black peak and to take her back to the purple patch.

But the other gray birds wanted them to stay. So it was another while of squawking and screeching, and only after the strange gray bird had promised to bring the beautiful fragile butterfly back to the black peak for another visit, before they were on their way.

And all of the strange gray birds they had visited were happy. They liked the beautiful fragile butterfly who tried to speak their language and they were happy that their friend was happy.

And the beautiful fragile butterfly was happy.

And the strange gray bird was happy.

And everyday the strange gray bird and the beautiful fragile butterfly visited with the other gray birds in the black peak. The other birds collected white flowers and brought them into the black peak so the beautiful fragile butterfly would have something to munch on and maybe feel more at home. And the strange gray bird who was her friend shaded her with his wing in the black peak. And the beautiful fragile butterfly told them all she had seen in the green land with the red flowers and in the brown land with the blue flowers and about the rain that was not rain but a sea. And the strange gray birds all squawked but they did not tell her about anywhere she did not already see.

And for a long time the beautiful fragile butterfly was happy visiting the gray birds in the black peak and resting in the purple patch on the tiny white flowers beneath the shade of the wing of the strange gray bird who was her friend, and visiting and resting and visiting and resting.

But one day, when the strange gray bird and the beautiful fragile butterfly had returned to the purple patch, the strange gray bird did not fly up to take his position above the beautiful fragile butterfly. "What is it?" she asked.

And the strange gray bird who was her friend replied, "Beautiful fragile butterfly, come to the black peak and live with me forever. I have never seen anything like you and I am very happy now. I will make you happy and you will be happier every day. Please, stay with me forever. We will travel far together and you can tell me what you see. And we will see all that we can see. Please, stay with me."

And the beautiful fragile butterfly sat on her tiny white flower in the purple patch, very quiet for a very long time.

At last, she sighed a deep sigh and said in the hideous sounding language she had learned from the strange gray bird who loved her, "You are very kind, and very gentle, and although I cannot eat worms or live in the black peak, I love you."

Then she smiled at the strange gray bird and her bespeckled wings radiated a brilliant light in the sun that never set. "I have seen what I could see" she said.

"And all I could see, is me."

About the Author

Joyce Bloom was born in Brooklyn, New York. She holds a Bachelor's degree in Liberal Arts from Brooklyn College; a Master's from NYU in Teaching English as a Second Language and attended SUNY Maritime College at Fort Schuyler where she studied in the Transportation Management Master's Program. She has lectured for organizations and corporations on the subjects of international shipping, negotiating and interpersonal communications. She has been writing since she was a child and has published an article with Mary Carpenter in *IDIOM* and a poem in *Machon Chana Wisdom*. This is her first book.